little Miss Late

by Roger Hargreaves

PSS!
PRICE STERN SLOAN

Late for this.

Late for that.

Little Miss Late was late for everything!

For instance.

Do you know where she spent last Christmas?

At home.

Earlybird Cottage!

But, do you know *when* she spent Christmas?

January 25th!

One month late!

For example.

Do you know when she did her spring cleaning at Earlybird Cottage?

In the summer!

Three months late!

For instance.

Do you know when she went on her summer vacation last year?

In December!

Six months late!

Earlybird Cottage was just down the road from where a friend of hers lived.

Little Miss Neat.

Little Miss Neat was out for an evening stroll last October when she looked over the hedge of Earlybird Cottage.

Little Miss Late was in the garden.

"Hello," called out Little Miss Neat. "What are you doing?"

"I thought I'd cut the grass!" replied Little Miss Late.

"I think," remarked Little Miss Neat, looking at the grass, "that you should have thought about that last April!"

"Tell you what," suggested Little Miss Neat. "Let's go shopping together tomorrow!"

"Good idea," agreed Little Miss Late.

"I'll meet you in town on the corner of Main Street tomorrow afternoon," said Little Miss Neat. "Two o'clock!"

"I'll be there," replied Little Miss Late.

The following afternoon, Little Miss Neat stood on the corner of Main Street at two o'clock.

Waiting for Little Miss Late.

She waited.

And waited.

And waited.

And waited some more.

Little Miss Late arrived.

"Sorry I'm a little bit late," she apologized.

"Sorry?" cried Little Miss Neat. "A little bit late? It's five o'clock and all the shops are closed!"

"Sorry," said Little Miss Late.

And that's what happened, all the time!

It happened when Little Miss Late decided to get a job.

Her first job was in a bank.

But the trouble was, by the time she arrived for work, the bank had closed for the day.

Every day!

"Sorry," she said.

They asked her to leave.

It happened at her second job, as a waitress in a restaurant.

Mr. Greedy came in for lunch.

He glanced at the menu.

"I'll have everything," he grinned. "Twice!"

He was still waiting to be served at seven o'clock.

So he went home.

"Sorry," said Little Miss Late.

They asked her to leave.

It happened at her third job, working as a secretary for Mr. Uppity.

"I'd like these letters typed before I go home," Mr. Uppity said to her.

He went home at four o'clock.

In the morning!

"Sorry," said Little Miss Late.

He asked her to leave.

However, as it happened, which is often the way of things, Little Miss Late managed to find herself the perfect job.

She now works for Mr. Lazy!

She cooks and cleans for him.

Cleaning his house every morning.

Cooking his lunch every lunchtime.

Now.

Mr. Lazy, being Mr. Lazy, doesn't get up in the mornings like you and I do.

He gets up in the afternoon!

And Little Miss Late, being Little Miss Late, is always late for work.

So she doesn't arrive for work in the morning.

She arrives in the afternoon!

And.

Mr. Lazy, being Mr. Lazy, doesn't have lunch at lunchtime like you and I do.

He has lunch at suppertime!

And so you see, it all works very well.

Very well indeed!

Last Friday evening, the telephone rang in Earlybird Cottage.

Little Miss Late had just arrived home from work.

It was Mr. Silly on the telephone.

"I've been given some tickets for a dance tomorrow night," he said. "Would you like to come?"

"Ooh, yes please," said Little Miss Late eagerly.

"Great," replied Mr. Silly. "I'll pick you up at seven o'clock!"

Last Saturday, Mr. Silly walked up the path to the front door of Earlybird Cottage.

He knocked.

"Come in," called a voice from upstairs.

Mr. Silly went in.

"Make yourself at home," called Little Miss Late from upstairs.

"I'll be down in a minute!"